ELOISE'S
GUIDE TO LIFE

KAY THOMPSON'S

ELOISE'S
GUIDE TO LIFE

OR HOW TO
EAT,
DRESS,
TRAVEL,
BEHAVE,
and
STAY SIX
FOREVER!

Drawings by
HILARY KNIGHT

Simon & Schuster Books for Young Readers

New York   London   Toronto   Sydney   Singapore

SIMON & SCHUSTER BOOKS FOR YOUNG READERS

An imprint of Simon & Schuster Children's Publishing Division

1230 Avenue of the Americas, New York, New York 10020

SIMON & SCHUSTER BOOKS FOR YOUNG READERS is a trademark of Simon & Schuster.

Manufactured in China

4 6 8 10 9 7 5

0311 SCP

Library of Congress Cataloging-in-Publication Data

Thompson, Kay, 1911-1998

Eloise's guide to life: or how to eat, dress, travel, behave & stay six forever / by Kay Thompson ; illustrated by Hilary Knight.—1st ed.

p. cm.

Excerpts from: Kay Thompson's Eloise: The Absolutely Essential Edition, Eloise in Paris, Eloise at Christmastime, and Eloise in Moscow.

Summary: A collection of quotations from the unconventional heroine of the Eloise books by Kay Thompson.

ISBN 0-689-83310-5

1. Thompson, Kay, 1911--Quotations—Juvenile literature. 2. Eloise (Fictitious character : Thompson)—Juvenile literature. 3. Conduct of life—Juvenile humor. [1. Conduct of life—Wit and humor. 2. Wit and humor.] I. Knight, Hilary, ill. II. Title.

PS3570.H642355 A6 2000

813'.54—dc21

99-046968

I pick up the phone and call Room Service

Langoustines make very good fingernails

Here's what I can do

Chew gum

You have to eat oatmeal or you'll dry up

Anybody knows that

An egg cup makes a very good hat

Toe shoes make very good ears

A melon makes a very good iced foot bucket and a very good heat-ray hat

If I pretend I am an orphan

they give me a piece of melon or something

HOW TO DRESS

The first thing you have to do

is put on your gloves

I put a large cabbage leaf on my head

when I have a headache

You can't even dine with your boots on in Moscow

We put on our woollies to protect

us from the freezing weather

My day is rawther full

I have to call the Valet and tell him

to get up here and pick up

my sneakers to be cleaned and pressed

Here's what I am

a clothes horse

I am always packed in case

I have to leave on TWA

at a moment's notice

or something like that

You absolutely have

to have your camera

ready at all times

Sometimes they turn out

Sabena is the only airline that will allow
you to travel with a turtle

We had 114 pieces of luggage

We had absolutely nothing to declare

If you do not understand
simply nod your head
and say "No Comprendo"

If you are going to Paris France

you have to turn into French

and go absolutely wild

Paris raindrops are larger

If there is a lot of rain and wet

simply go to the Louvre

Froid is right

Chaud is left

and you can count on it practically all of the time

but not always

You absolutely cannot go

anywhere in Paris

without your map

 Here's what they have a lot of in Paris

pigeons

Here's the thing of it

Most of the time I'm on the telephone

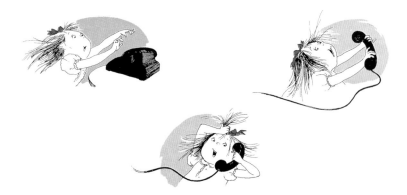

Here's what you can do while you're waiting

look around a lot

or you can play with your face a little

If you are a diplomat here is what is not possible

snowballs

I go to as many holiday parties

as I possibly can

Give a Christmas stocking at Christmastime

Skipperdee dislikes peppermint puffs and

won't even smell the fudge

Oh my Lord I am absolutely so busy I don't know
how I can possibly get everything done

Sometimes there is so much to do that

I get sort of a headache around the sides

and partially under it

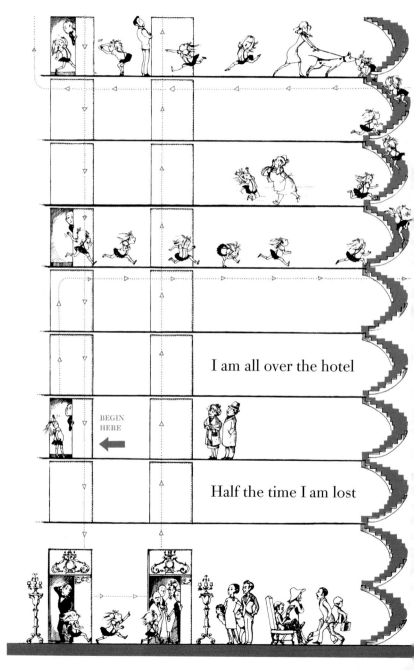

BEGIN HERE

I am all over the hotel

Half the time I am lost

Getting bored is

not allowed

Here's what I like to do

Make things up

Paper cups are very good for talking to Mars

Sometimes I

have a

temper fit

But not very often

I make as much noise as I possibly can

DON'T DISTURB

You can hum with your eyes closed and no one will hear you

Sometimes I put a rubber band

on the end of my nose

I have a turtle

His name is Skipperdee

The Plaza is the only hotel in New York
that will allow you to have a turtle

I have a dog that looks like a cat

Sometimes I comb my hair

with a fork

Sometimes I take a nap

and forget where I am

Oh

I could tell you a lot

but I am only six